CEREALISM

I0600193

by
Shawn Misener

ROADSIDE PRESS

Cover Art: Ray Swaney
Editor: Michele McDannold

Roadside Press
Meredosia, Illinois

Table of Contents

What a wicked thing to do, to make me dream of you.
—Chris Isaak, "Wicked Game"

Mastery of All Thangs Including Sonatas and Piledrivers

I'm suddenly virtuosic on the piano. You may think I look a little silly with a shaved and sprayed body, glistening even in the subdued aura of candlelight, rippling muscles tight and focused on the keys and footpedals, but I don't feel silly. The black speedo, tiny denim vest, and fully-groomed mullet may not pair well with a sonata, I realize this, but it's not like I chose this destiny. At least not on this night.

It feels great to be in this kind of shape. I could be a sex machine if I wanted to be, a real lovemaking jackhammer, but so far there's no sign of any women. I close my eyes and try to will one into existence, a kind of mash-up of every crush I've ever had, sprinkled with Lebanese, but it doesn't work. There are limits, even though I couldn't tell you what they are.

My old buddy Snoop Dogg saunters into the room, and we go through a handshake routine that takes over ten minutes, ending with double-backflips and some brotherly penis swordplay.

"Damn Snoop, did you get your shit extended?" I ask, popping my pecs.

"Naw Homey, I got it expandified." Snoop leaves his package out as display.

"Awww Yeah!" I blurt, not knowing what the hell he means.

Eventually we get ourselves clothed again, and I step back on the baby grand, accompanied by some unbelievable beatboxing on Snoop's part. Our musical synergy feels so good, so right, that I find myself whoopin' and hollerin' and almost losing control of my incredibly buff body.

Andre the Giant crashes through the ceiling, and we immediately stop the jam in order to tend to his wounds, but he lifts himself up and brushes the dust off of his saggy nipples. "Keep playing," he urges us. "I came here to rap with you."

I can hardly contain my excitement, being in a trio with Snoop and Andre. What? WHAT? IT'S FUCKING AWESOME. I AM FUCKING AWESOME AT THE PIANO. I AM FUCKING AWESOME PERIOD.

After several hours of jamming—concluding with an unbelievably tight rendition of "Kasmir"—we hug and jump around and giggle like little girls. These guys are my bests friends EVER.

I ask Andre and Snoop if they know where the ladies are, and they look at me all confused, like they don't understand the question.

"Women?" I reiterate. "Females? Do you know what I'm talking about?"

"It's cool, it's cool," Snoop says. "You need me to give you a blowjob?"

"You're missing the point," I whimper.

Andre flops down on the couch next to me, which sends me about ten feet into the air. I land on his lap and he strokes my hair. "It's ok, little one," he says. "I will make you feel better." I can sense his gigantic hand creeping into my underwear, like a clumsy tarantula.

I suddenly remember that I'm a badass wrestler, so I go about throwing Snoop out of the stained-glass window, and then body slamming Andre ala Hulk Hogan at Wrestlemania 3. It quickly becomes a carnage, as nameless people start coming at me from all sides. I dispatch them easily, one at a time, for what seems like hours. It's a little like playing the piano; the less I think about it, the easier it is to break their bodies and send them out the window.

When the dust settles I clap the dust off my hands, yell "WOOOO!" and lean over the balcony. The pile of bodies is impressive. Slowly, like a confused ant finding his way out of a pile of wet woodchips, Snoop emerges from the tangle of limbs and torsos, holding up a lit joint and smiling. "Get your ass down here, this ain't gonna smoke itself!"

Cactus Subconscious

I'm bouncing along the desert like a rubber ball, deftly avoiding cactus after angry cactus. My pants are soaked with scorpion juice.

The voice in the sand: "If it has soul you must funk it."

The field of geysers has turned to carbonation. A bubbling tribute to the three clouds suspended in the air. What does a cloud feel like when swallowed?

Below, the army of Southwestern poets begins to gather. One by one they set up shop: Rusty typewriters, old booze, loose tobacco, and pissy attitudes. Flailing through the sky I see them as they skeptically measure me up.

"He won't be up there for long," they croak, sharing nods and commiserating huffs. The clacking of atomic words explodes from their fingers. They blast away my abstractions with sex, drugs, and indie rock.

"See you when you fall," they sing.

The Tour(ette's) Guide

This is my sixteenth glass of orange juice, and the sixteenth glass that has shattered before I can lift it to my mouth. These dry and quivering lips have grown impatient and are threatening to spew expletives in Portuguese.

I am of course naked, my skin sticky sweet and matted with pulp. The walls are on fire, as they should be, my frustration turning dragon. There is a woman in here—I am never alone—but she is fully clothed in Detroit Derby Dolls gear and stands at a modest seven inches tall.

I turn to her and sigh, "Are you the one doing this to me?"

She cackles like a demon, her bellow cutting through the smoke. "Who the fuck do you think I am? That chick from The Hunger Games? Legolas? Cupid? Any old coot with a bow and arrow?"

"I think you are some kind of evil bitch, and I would appreciate it if you crawled up my ass now."

She languidly sits at the edge of the coffee table and dangles her bruised legs in a violently playful rhythm.

"Hmmm," she muses. "Back where I came from?"

"Back where you came from," I hiss, nodding imperceptibly.

The south wall crumbles from the flames, thousands of neon embers billowing up and settling into constellations above us. I find myself standing, with a new glass of juice in one hand, the other one flailing behind me, trying to grab her. She is suddenly normal size, no, bigger than that, a freakish giant, squatting behind me and working her forearm into my anus.

A disturbingly unreal scream escapes me in the form of a cacophony of cuckoo clocks chiming all at once... underwater. The glass again shatters and I use both hands in a poor attempt to extract her from inside me.

Her voice smashes into my earholes: "HOW FAR WE HAVE COME, HOW FAR WE CAN GO, I'M IN THIS SHIT, UP TO MY ELBOW."

And she's in. The world feels perfect again, clean, delineated by straight lines and Febreeze.

I'm sitting on the couch, watching the fireplace and thinking that maybe this was the most symmetrical and pleasing wood stacking job I've ever accomplished. The fire seems content with its balance. The pictures of my eight children smile back at me, so evenly spaced, so full of goodness. I resist the urge to rearrange them in alphabetical order. The first week of the month is always by age, the second by melatonin concentration, the third by income, and not until next week do they line up by name.

I slowly swallow the orange juice, wishing I had a straw to protect my teeth from the acid. When I belch, it's her laughing. She wants me to check the lock on the door. She wants me to shout random words. She wants me to blink and blink and blink and blink. She wants me to execute the tic where I rub my eyebrows until they bleed.

"COCKSUCKER! TERRIFIC PIZZA! COCKSUCKER!" I yell, jumping from the couch to the rug. I know that she's satisfied, somewhere in there. She's satisfied as hell and she has a cool grip on my thalamus.

Broadcast From Earth Deli

In case of accidental data explosion ignore the slowly dispersing fractal pattern of my history. Too much attention to reality will lead to digital self-realization, and we can't be having any of THAT. Observe the fragments of the me with a careful eye tuned to a station of ignorance. I'm only here—and just barely here at that—because we all signed pre-gestational agreements to pretend existence exists. The only reality that broadcasts at this hour (and epoch) is the story of non-reality, which makes perfect sense because nothing's perfect and it's sensical nonsense that makes the most sense.

A man walks into a bar and becomes Manbar, hero of our times. He winds the clocks and develops humans in drunken fits. He might look like God, what with the massive white beard and body the size of New Hampshire, but don't let him fool you. Everyone in power is not in control. He's just Manbar, a meaty sandwich type who wears watches all the way up to his redwood bicep. Nice throaty bellow, to be sure, but volume is no way to measure omnipresence. And what he does with souls can easily be replicated by a platypus with play-doh and a Sanskrit translator.

As you finish scooping up my past remnants tune the moments down to 27 bps and then turn to Manbar. Be confident, and regardless of your empty skull speak the Word to him. When the rumbling starts, you'll know it's time to make me into I for the last and first time.

I have no confidence that you'll complete the task. Shit, you probably don't even understand it in the slightest. Fine. I'm dust, forever wiggling free and hollow in space, making the best of it. It isn't what it isn't, like they never say.

Smoking Giants

There's smoke coming out of the cave. People gawk and flutter by me on the pier, safe from harm. Agitated voices agitating me. Raising up the ghosts of frightened chickens.

"Can you see into it?" a man asks behind me.

"Too dark." I begin, turning, but he's not there anymore. I wonder if he was ever there at all.

It started out thin and directed, as if maybe a giant crouched with his giant-sized cigarette. Now it's more. A crowd of giants, smoking the place out.

The cackling is gone from the pier. I watch them, an amoeba of humans, moving away from the cave. They leave a languorous trail on the beach. I think they've always been together, talking amongst themselves about whatever is happening around them. A part of me wishes they'd walk into the cave and disturb whatever is burning it from the inside out.

I find a cigarette in the breast pocket of my shirt. I haven't smoked in months, or years even. Maybe if I hold it up to the mouth of the cave it'll light. It's only perception that the pier where I stand is hundreds of yards from the fire. The fire I can't see. The fire I can't see getting bigger, creating more and more smoke.

I slip the butt end in my mouth and line up the tip to the cave. Inhale. I can't hear the people anymore. For now it's just the cave and the pier. And me, smoking again.

Toad on Fire

People always remarked that his voice sounded like a muscle car. "Idle or rolling?" he would ask, lighting cigarettes and squinting. "Seriously though, how many people have to tell me that before I start slaughtering?"

Brenda glanced at the trees, the relaxed park-goers, the sneaky bugs fluttering between scenes and most likely considering themselves to be invisible. If they considered themselves at all. The sentience of insects was a suspect notion, she thought, not even worth the five seconds she was giving it. She smashed a voyaging ant under her thumb to prove the point. I don't feel guilty at all, she mused.

The sun was gracious and kept behind the clouds. They stood and stretched and silently stared at each other, silly human beings they were. Eventually she spoke: "You rev. Vroom vroom."

"I guess so," he conceded, hands in pockets.

"This is, I don't know, like an arthouse film or something," she said.

"Totally pretentious," he added.

"Totally."

The drugs were good. No, they were the best. Hamrick the Dealer had informed her that—like all quality narcotics—she would find herself looking down on everything. Becoming a third person. She shared the little pills with Clive so they could both be narrators. It was a noble and pretentious idea.

"Where are we going?" he asked as they slid between two thorny bushes. "Machete: Activate"

With an ear-popping SCHVING he came to possess a large blade and wasted no time in using it to clear a path through the hostile shrubbery.

"Be careful with that, hombre," she said. His arcs and swipes were a bit too much on the loose side for her. "Have you ever used one of those before?"

"Absolutely not."

"I would like to keep my head, at least for a few more nights. Didn't you say we were gonna have sex one of these days? Isn't that in the manual?"

He slowly turned around, completely conscious of the dramatic effect such a methodical swivel would produce. He let a few stray thorns carve into his biceps and form squiggly blood patterns around his tattoos. It was all in good fun. And it was rousing the right response from her: Her breathing became ragged and desperate, her eyes glazed over and quivered briefly, she unconsciously began twisting her hair around her fingers. "Mmmmm..." he growled, batting his eyes and smacking his lips.

"Mmmmm?" she replied.

"Mmmmm," he confirmed, and they both fell into the bushes, propelled by the force of their sudden unstoppable laughter. The glee quickly turned to howls of pain. After all, these were thorn bushes.

It felt as though her body was overtaken by a thousand points of suffering, and she immediately fell into a sort of willful coma. Moving only made it worse. She could feel the thorns in her eyeballs, her lips, her ears, her breasts, her toes. Everywhere.

Clive screamed in an epic baritone, scaring off the crows that had gathered to document their LOVE EFFORTS. They collectively mourned such a waste of narrative promise.

He thoughtlessly flailed the machete, which didn't do much to release him from the bushes. Instead, two extremely unfortunate outcomes played out: The thorns that were already embedded in his skin slid even deeper, in some cases making contact with bone and vital organs. And, much to his dismay, he beheaded Brenda.

At this point he also opted for a willful coma instead of witnessing the rich geyser of blood that was blasting from her neck. The crows returned, recording devices on again, aware that it no longer was a LOVE EFFORT, but instead a FATAL TRAGEDY. They could hardly contain their joy, and the songs they bellowed could be heard for miles in all directions.

When Clive regained consciousness the bushes were gone, Brenda was gone, the park was gone, shit everything was gone from what had seemed like a solid setting just moments before. Instead he was reclining in a large purple bean bag in an empty kindergarten classroom. He recognized the teacher pacing before him as Mrs. Ballard. She had his machete.

"This is a nice one, Clive," she said, turning it over

and examining it. "No flaws, correct dimensions... really good work for a novice such as yourself. I even got a chance to see the way you swing it. The birds got a few good angles in. Except for the overly-dramatic severing of Brenda's head your form is impeccable."

"So that really happened."

"What kind of question is that? Think about it. It went from a love story to a tale of lifetime regret like that," she snapped her fingers. "Sometimes, with people like you, I wonder if you really know what's going on."

Mrs. Ballard began undressing. "Is this what you want? Are we gonna fuck right here, on the alphabet mat?" Off came the skirt, the blouse, the bra, the panties. She was moving too fast and he could see her image becoming skittish. Bad transmission.

"She suggested it to me. She wanted to have sex. Remember?"

"No," she said, her voice crackling. Her left arm was suddenly missing. "You both wanted it. It was in your manual."

"My manual," he remembered.

Mrs. Ballard was only a mouth by now, with a sliver of nose hovering inches above and spinning wildly. "My god," she (the mouth) breathed. "You have a terribly sexy voice. It almost sounds like a motorcycle on idle."

"Don't say that," he murmured.

"Oh, but I did," the mouth said, biting at his belt. "I know where the story starts, and I know where the story ends."

"Where's that?"

Instead of replying the mouth focused its efforts into yanking down the zipper to his jeans. Clive watched, resigned and exasperated, as the spinning nose exploded like a rocket and became lodged in the ceiling.

"Oops," said the mouth. "Remind me to get that back later."

"When it's over?"

"Yes, Clive, when it's over."

The Baby with Monster Truck Wheels

The baby has no legs. Just monster truck wheels.

She rolls around the yard, fifteen feet high. Nine months old, such amazing control.

Grandpa sets up some things for her to crush. The old Gremlin. Al's doghouse. That dilapidated barn.

Baby has the spirit. We can hear her cooing from down here. Under the porch.

We start to wonder if the electric fence can hold her in. She's taken to killing the sheep and sucking them up with a drain pipe. The once cute baby noises now sound monstrous.

Somebody needs to call Frank. The pediatrician who fixes cars on the side.

If there's a storm rolling in we might be able to make a break for it. She's bound to run out of gas one of these days.

Beasts of the Talent Show

The crowd of parents is stuffed into an empty sand-box and forced to watch the talent show. One by one our children are paraded out riding various species of wildlife: The twins on matching chimpanzees, the Thai kid on a skittish giraffe, a terrified looking boy dressed in rags clinging to the neck of a limping os-trich. I can hardly draw breath from the center of the pulsing throng of adults.

Finally my daughter emerges from behind the silver curtain, riding piggy-back on a gigantic proboscis monkey. She's preoccupied by his nose, and wrings it like a wet dishrag with both hands. If it hurts he's not showing it.

The animals dutifully form a chorus line in front of the suffocating parents. They begin a rhythmic series of bellows, grunts, chirps, howls, and other odd beast noises. Above this natural backbeat of wildlife the children launch into the first verse of Jethro Tull's "Rumble in the Jungle."

It's oddly beautiful.

The swarm of parents is becoming too much. I can

feel the sweat of at least four different people dropping onto my neck and shoulders. The fat guy in front of me farts against my hip.

Eventually the song ends and the parents rush the stage, full of anger and screaming at the animals. Released from the prison of aging flesh and bodily functions I fall to my knees and catch my breath. I watch as they snatch their kids from their rides, toss them behind, and begin to wail on the creatures, who don't seem to have the energy to fight back.

My daughter jogs over to me, pulling the reluctant monkey by the nose behind her. "Aren't you going to kill it?" she asks.

The parents have begun piling the dead animals up. One of them produces a jug of gasoline and lights the pyre. "Dinner, motherfuckers!" he screams, full of savage energy.

I examine the monkey, who stares back at me with dumb, resigned eyes. The adults have set up a make-shift picnic table and are setting out paper plates and pitchers of Kool-Aid. A particularly heavy father, the grillmaster, brandishes an impossibly large fork and and manipulates the pile of burning animals, digging out pounds of random meats and stacking them on the plates of salivating adults and kids.

"Not for us," I say to my daughter. We walk away, the three of us holding hands. Child, proboscis monkey, parent.

"Is this the peaceful option, Daddy?"

"It's either this or that vulgar display."

"Oh."

The monkey stops walking and turns to face us. He appears worn and when he speaks the words are barely audible: "My gratitude to you is immeasurable, kind sir. Where the rest of your fellow humans chose the immediate pleasures of murder and gluttony, you chose love. And when you elevate love over all else, you prove your enlightenment. Here, take this as a token of my infinite indebtedness."

He reaches around his backside, grunts, and offers me a fresh pile of monkey shit.

"Ewwww!" My daughter moans.

I'm not sure what to do, so I shrug and continue walking. My daughter scurries up to my side, leaving the monkey standing with poop in his outstretched hand.

"Just fling it somewhere," I say.

The dull sound of shit splatting against grass. We don't look back to see if the monkey is following.

Popcorn Tigers

There are so many couches.

They stretch to the horizon, and for a moment I feel trapped in an Art Van, until I realize that I am not indoors. I am in the Sahel. The earth is cracked beneath me and the air wavers with heat rising from the leather padding on the seats

There are tigers in the distance. They leap over the couches deftly, slowly leaving the sun behind and targeting me. There must be a dozen of them.

I would run, but between my legs a gigantic green elephant rests, chortling from deep inside his chest. I implore him to flee by pulling on his ears but he ignores me and continues his gruff laugh. I am high enough to escape the tigers but cannot contain my fear. They are only a few couches away now.

The last row of furniture is all black leather. In unison the tigers hop onto a couch a piece, sit calmly on their haunches, and reach for remote controls buried in the cushions. Roaring, they paw at the remotes.

The elephant is by now almost crying with laughter.

Dull clicks pop in the air around me. The elephant is rapidly changing colors as fast as the tigers can change the channel. Green, red, blue, grey, purple, pink...they don't stop tapping the remote. The tigers join the elephant in uproarious laughter.

I realize that I am the only one not getting the humor. The tiger closest to me looks up and sighs. "Chill out my friend," he says. "We're about to make popcorn."

Apocalypse w/ Giraffes

It went down but normal language can't describe it. Yellow steam puffed out like aerosol from tiny holes in the land. The planet began spinning and farting across the universe. Many creatures died that first day, unable to hold on. Me, I found a sturdy mangrove to wrap myself in.

So I was saved. At times, I wish I wasn't.

I'm constantly having glass surface conversations with disabled giraffes under the trees. They clue me in, like private reporters. One of them said that home is nothing more than a big deflating piece of shit. The proboscis monkey had to concur.

I found my dad a while back, floating through the swamp next to the coffee-maker and bowtie deposits. He instructed me to give up hope. Give it up quick.

Time is like a memory from the womb. Who knows how long I have been crouched here, tied down by kelp and thin vines, trading laments with animals? They all look terrified.

Her Head Sounserals Away

He screws on his hat until it clicks into place. His child's head is loose and keeps sliding off the neck pole. He tries seven times to secure her head into place, but as soon as she starts toddling it wobbles for a bit then falls to the carpet and bounces away.

He sees a lot of things that there are no words for. He wonders if, in other languages, they have words for them.

The movement of his child's plastic head as it sashays/bounces/spirals away, what do you call that? Sounseral. Sounseral! Her head sounserals away, into the dark closet.

Once her head is on for good he carries her onto the balcony, and they are speaking in a tongue he's never heard. He has no idea what they are saying to each other. But they seem happy enough, lots of smiles.

They sound like two Swedish Chefs, one big and with a deep, comforting voice, the other small and possessing the squeals and honks of a large bird. "Bortste fornert de dort!" he says, bouncing her.

"Bortne! Bortne! Shushort!" she exclaims, shooting her hands over her wobbly head in pleasure, causing it to again pop off. This time, it's a three story drop from a balcony.

Terrified, he yells "Sneeeeew nuuuu! Oh nee padoooo!"

Her head rolls into the deep grass. The grass is neon yellow, like shredded cheddar. Her detached head makes it's way, rolling from stalk to stalk, chewing contentedly. He's never seen her so happy. He hears a muffled "Booboonoo!" from the tall grass, and smiles as her headless body, which he is still holding, gives him two thumbs up.

Robots Make Our Food

"This is where we suck the skin off the beasts," remarks the General, pointing to a small white tube dangling from the ceiling. "We coat the mouthpiece with mushroom sauce, and as soon as they wrap their stinky bulbous lips around it...VROOOP! No more skin."

He leads us over to an electrified holding pen, where several skinned beasts meander, bouncing off one another and yelping squeamishly. The General smiles and points to them with his bone cane. "These are the skinless sows. Watch what happens when I press this button." He taps a tiny button with the cane and the floor releases, sending the beasts into the void with the force of a public restroom toilet. Rousing applause booms from speakers mounted on the fence.

"Thank you, thank you," says the General, bowing.

The tiny pink woman touring with me pipes up, "Isn't it the truth, Herr General, that robots make our food? What do you say to that?"

"You bitch!" He sings, pounding the top of her bald head with his cane. "Where do you think you are?

Afmenistan? Turkily? This is 'Merica! We invented robots." Breathing deeply and adjusting his robes, he whistles. The entire facility rumbles upon the grand entrance of a metallic ball the size of a three-story Victorian. It saunters up next to us, and I feel compelled to hop the fence and join the beasts in their doom.

The General laughs. "This what happens when you roll all the robots into one! A Katamari! You guys want some dinner?"

This Rubbery, Unsure Thing

The sea is transparent rubber, and peering down into it I recognize the shiny fish in suspended animation, their partially exploded bodies obscured by their own blood. The appearance of flecks and trails of color solidified in a newly minted marble. I stand above them and test the buoyancy of the water, and find that it is nothing less than a trampoline, extending to the horizon in all directions.

The ocean is dead. A divine snapshot must have fated the water and its inhabitants to this. A solid jelly that no ship will ever cross and no fisherman will ever drop his lure into. What a cruel fucking twist of events, I think aloud. Above, the clouds continue on their slow roll, muting the sun and releasing it in turn, and I find myself thinking of my children. I can't remember their names, or how many there are, but hot fury wells up from my abdomen when I think of them potentially playing in the waves one moment, then the next frozen in this fucking rubber. Dead eyes open and enthused, locked in place in the act of swimming behind a rambling crab, all fates suddenly equal.

So I bounce. It doesn't matter which direction. At

twenty feet into the sky I flatten out and take in the panorama. Schools of tiny fish, now laminated into twisting swirls that again remind me of marbles. The larger residents of this absurdity—the sharks and jellyfish—dotting the field like a scatter plot. I let my body hit the water face down, arms wide. The surface gives and an absurdly wretched sucking fills my ears, and my mouth is instantly pried open by the jelly. I can feel it hardening against my tongue, my eardrums, and even my ass. There won't be any more breathing.

I look down at what amounts to the portrait that I will carry with me into death. The ocean floor is only a few yards down, though I was sure it wasn't visible before. And there they are, my children. All ten of them, sitting cross legged in a circle, their necks tilted back enough that I can see the color of their eyes and the curved frowns of their lips. There is no sound but I can hear them screaming, their violent cries bouncing behind my eyes. I scream back at them, knowing fully what terror is composed of. It's not the fear of death, it IS death. Terror is reserved for those who are dead already, but have yet to succumb. The realization that there is only this last moment before everything is stolen away into the blackness.

I pull back on the stick and lift the plane a bit. A quiet voice through the headset: "Daddy, can we go home now?"

"Yeah."

The ocean still churns under us. I wonder what would happen if I just shut down all the systems and let the Cessna glide gently down into the water. I can see the look on my son's face as the water fills the cabin, the usual confidence he has in my eternal heroism overtaken by panic. Would he realize then that nothing is to be taken for granted?

Setting the trajectories toward the airport I feel the first real thing I've felt in ages. The ebb and flow of being a living, breathing human fucking BEING. The on and off nature of consciousness. I'm taking us home and below the ocean is roiling, yet we are still dead, dead, dead, solidified like ancient bugs in a surreal rubber, our last moments spent admiring the sweeping pattern of hundreds of little fish, frozen in time.

Gazpacho

It's a pretty strange feeling when you think you're about to bite into some ice cream and instead it's gazpacho. I winced and moaned and watched her walk back toward the kitchen. She was so so serious when she said "You need to pay closer attention to things." Nevermind. The news was on the television and some dark-skinned rebels were running through clouds of smoke. Children carted away on stretchers made of blasted shards of drywall. Outside the ice cream man was in full Doppler, coming then going, and I entertained the notion of tossing the disgusting cold soup on the floor and making a break for it. It's just not possible to have everything I want.

She was either laughing or crying hunched over the kitchen sink. We were sick with humidity. I went for beers in the fridge, gently touching her hips in passing. She waved me off. "What's the matter?" I asked, not actually caring, popping open the beer and drinking most of it in one tip. "Like you fucking give a shit." That was it, she was crying. I shook my head and told her that the soup wasn't so bad after all, even though I knew I wouldn't touch it before sneaking it into the disposal later.

Three days later and she was gone. It only took a few minutes to toss out all of the moldy things in the fridge, including her gazpacho. I almost didn't. For a brief and torturous moment I could sense her presence locked up in the Tupperware, like some twisted and desperate ghost, but the sentimentality was gone before it came and I proceeded to open the lid on the ice cream.

A Leg and a Leg and Another Leg

A toddler sidles up next to me and wraps her chunky arms around my leg. She's trying to move me somewhere, possibly Montana, but I'm not going anywhere until I finish programming this robot.

It occurs to me that, not unlike the grunting child, I've also got my arms wrapped around a leg. The robot is taller than a modest oak. I wonder if something has its arms around the toddler's leg, something I can't see. And if that thing has something attached to its leg, and so forth, down into cellular levels. The other way, too: The robot may be grabbing onto something so big I'm mistaking it for the countryside, or the sunset. I could just be one cog in an infinite chain of leg-attachment, stretching from the cosmos to the sub-atomic. And, if I manage to finally program this robot, and he begins his prescribed itinerary to most distant pharmacies, how will that affect the toddler's plans for me?

Never mind, the job is done. I slap one more button into place, press it down for exactly three seconds, and the robot's motor kicks into gear. "Let's go," it booms. I forget to let go, and suddenly I'm swinging back and forth as he trudges across the prairie. It reminds me of those pirate ship rides at the fair, except I'm not strapped in and at any second I could lose my handle and fall to my death.

The toddler's grip on my leg is tourniquet-tight. "Hang on!" I scream down to her. She seems to be gaining distance on me, my leg is psychedelically stretching down a thousand yards to the ground. I look up for the robot and only see the sun...Or is that his crotch? Suddenly I am unsure, existentially unsure. Am I the robot, being built? Or am I the toddler, hanging on for dear life to the adult who seems to be made of taffy?

Regardless, legs are swaying, and everybody is moving. Just keep hanging on, I tell myself. Hang on, go, arrive.

Banana Cream Pies For Sixty Percents

She's talking to me about solar flares. There are so many words that I can't make out, even though she is standing right in front of me. I think that on some meta-level we have bad transmission.

It's bone quiet in the desert yet her words come at me through an invisible storm. She doesn't seem to notice that I can't understand her. I hear THE SUN and ELECTRICITY and MOTHER and GHOSTS. I hear SOLAR FLARES a few times. She is smiling. I know somehow that her name is Bobbi.

Suddenly the auditory havoc dies down and she falls into a loop, saying BANANA CREME PIES FOR SIXTY PERCENTS over and over.

I find my drums half-buried in the next dune over and play a funky beat over her ongoing vocal sample. There is a juice welling up inside of my gut.

My cell phone rings and it's James Brown looking for Kenny G. I peer around the horizon but I can't find the curly-maned soprano saxophonist. Bobbi continues looping on about the pies.

For a terrible second I realize that the desert is infinite, and that means death.

The aroma of coffee seeps through the cracks, followed in by the crying of an infant.

Harvesting Brains Pastoral

The sky is red and violent and the skinny farmer digs up brains with his shovel.

Pitching them from the earth they shriek in Morse code. A bawdy secretary languishes behind the farmer, translating the squealing gray matter and scratching her rectangular nose obsessively.

As each rusted wheelbarrow fills with minds a donkey appears and slouches away with the load. "Fourteen thousand eight hundred and twenty seven" counts the secretary in whispers born under the prairie wind.

Somewhere behind the far distant trees a monstrous fog horn bellows. Both the farmer and the secretary vanish in identical puffs of heavy dust, leaving behind brains strewn around like so much neglected cauliflower.

A vacuous, slow moment.

Then a new farmer appears, the atmosphere popping violently in his arrival, followed by another short-skirted secretary, her glasses askew and eyes cocked in confusion.

The second shift begins when the farmer scoops his first brain. The sky reluctantly shades from maroon to a painful deep purple, the clouds wrench themselves into loose threatening coils, and the secretary bends an elven ear towards the multitudes of pleading encephalitic vegetables.

The Sauce

Asked to describe my work history I reach into my man-purse and pull out a live octopus. Placing him on the table between us the supervisor seems pleased. He investigates the creature from multiple angles, often using his pencil to poke at a tentacle or an eyeball.

I begin singing "Octopus' Garden", and both the supervisor and the octopus join in. I'm surprised that our harmony is near-perfect.

Suddenly we are all driven silent. The room is shaking from what feels like a massive earthquake. The supervisor, sensing the fear in me, pats my hand and says "Never you mind! This is normal in the tomato. Every few days we rile up, make sauce, and regrow again. Have you ever been in spaghetti sauce before?"

The octopus rolls inconspicuously off the table and lands on the carpet with a farting noise. "So I guess I just wait," I mumble.

"Yes, yes, you wait," the supervisor intones, smiling and tapping his fingers against his substantial gut.

Red Lady Octopus

We're in my kitchen, except it's not really my kitchen.

She is painted red and glowing faintly. Short, she blends into the armpits and ribs of the chatting men around her. They give her no notice and continue sloshing their cocktails around, drenching her in soda.

She emits a light buzz, and I want to wrap my arms around her just to find out from where inside her the hum originates, but I think of my wife and keep my distance.

I realize that the four or five guys—who may or may not be my friends—are speaking in gibberish, like records being pushed backward against their wills.

I open the fridge and look for cheese. There is only a live octopus, imploring me to throw it out the window. I want to oblige, but the men have drawn closer, surrounding me in Old Spice.

I hand one of them the octopus and run out of the room.

The Deadly Cake Forest

All of the trees are made of cake, and depending on the kind of tree, a different kind of cake. The kids are happy at this astounding revelation. To all of them except for Alex (a certified nature enthusiast) trees were boring pieces of shit that were good for the occasional reckless climb and nothing else. Now they are delicious and spongy.

They look like amateur beavers, all twenty-seven of them on their knees, gnawing through frosting bark. My wife is taking notes on a huge purple flower, listening to the kids as they shout out what tree corresponds to what flavor. In the case of a confusing or borderline tree she personally takes a bite herself. The elms are cherry, the holly are dark chocolate, the birch are lemon, and so on and so on.

It isn't long before I realize that pretty much every tree in the known universe is represented in this particular forest, and that there is only one of each tree. No regard to climate zones or any other known distinction.

"This is a fucking trap," I whisper to my wife. "Somebody planted these things to lure our kids in."

"Oh, don't be silly. I hate it when you get all conspiratorial." She shakes her head and wanders away with her giant flower notepad, following the random bellows of our children's discoveries.

But my hesitations prove correct. With a thunderous smash a black beaver the size of a hippo falls from somewhere above. Rising on two legs, it laughs in a deafening, evil baritone. "STUPID FUCKING HUMANS! ALWAYS A PREY TO CAKE!"

I lift a finger in the air as if to make a point, but it's useless. I'm not sure what point to make. Ten more gigantic beavers thud onto the forest floor, snatching up my children and crunching their bones with yellow teeth the size of manila folders. My wife tries to fend one off with her flower but is sent flying out of the picture by a casual and deadly beaver tail. In a matter of seconds all of the kids are mashed up and piled neatly in the center of the beavers, who appear to be holding a religious ritual. The smallest one, who is still comparable to a reliable old milk cow, is splashing frankincense throughout the proceedings with a shiny thurible.

He's singing the one Enya song I know.

Where Have You Gone, Honey Bear?

I love you almost as much as I love the frozen food aisle. My heart palpitates every time I close a glass freezer door and watch as it fogs over. I swell with joy when pizza goes on sale and I eat nothing else for an entire week.

Your love is like a rail of fluorescent lights, so sturdy, so illuminating, so reliable. You light my path to the deli counter.

When I wake up and look to my left, will you be there with me, snoring like an asthmatic bear? Or will it be the sixteen bags of sliced roast beef I purchased last night in a fit of ecstasy? That's the thrill of it, the not knowing.

Where have you gone, Honey Bear?

Collision

You think the black hole is out there, somewhere distant, unattainable, light years away. You also think it's a hole in space, where anything that enters vanishes forever.

Yet I know something. That black hole isn't really a hole. It's a condensed mass, a violent object, and if you look closely, it's RIGHT HERE. I can look in your eyes and see it, so clearly.

Take my heart, take my own black hole, and slam it against yours. See what happens.

A Truthful Possum

There's a talking possum sitting crosslegged at the top of the stairs, the light from the purple and green stained-glass window above cloaking him in peaceful hues.

"You will never love yourself. You are condemned to loathing all of your parts, no matter how glorious they may be. Look at your legs! They tremble, like twigs on a washing machine. Look at your eyes! They seek to deceive. Look at your teeth! They are better served as gambler's bones."

I look down at my chest, an open window. The lines are clean, no blood, no sign of a sternum.

"Look at your heart! It is nothing but a plastic mold. Your life is a reproduction of a reproduction. One in a line of millions!"

The possum is sneering with truth. I can smell the blood under his fingernails. He has seen it all, the backwoods distilleries and the back porch propane grilles. He has slept under the beds of whores and kings alike.

I remove my heart after struggling with the packaging. "Take it then," I gasp, underhanding it up the stairs. It bounces nonchalantly off his skull as he slips into meditation.

Seven-Fingered Save

Believe me, I would run if I could, but there seems to be a low haze of molasses clinging to my ankles.

The axe murderer is still hidden by the fog, yet I can hear his boots as they trudge a few yards behind. He's singing Brtiney Spears in a chipmunk voice and keeping the rhythm by swishing his weapon back and forth through the swamp.

Hit me baby one more time...There's something ahead, some neon blue haze mutating and reaching out from the condensation, a wild and rambunctious cousin to the fog, a wobbly blob of funky color. As I slog forward the shape gains form: Jesus himself, replete in a shimmering powder bathrobe and dancing the shuffle, his smile delineated by a thin line of black lipstick.

I suddenly wish I had been baptized, that my parents hadn't been eco-terrorists, that I hadn't stolen that candy bar from Wal-Mart three years ago, that I hadn't had so much unmarried sexual congress. Behind me the axe murderer screams like somebody's jammed two bratwurst in his eyes. His singing is done for the night.

Jesus holds out his right hand, beckoning me to approach with seven fingers. The weight has lifted from my legs, and I'm doing cartwheels in space, laughing like a maniac.

All Boys' Dreams

I'm in the back of math class, openly masturbating. I really don't want to be masturbating, but I can't seem to help myself.

Mr. Smith, who died three years ago, is passing out a test. I have no idea what the test is about, only that it's surely math, and I haven't studied at all. I'm destined to fail.

As Bull Smith approaches my secluded desk, I try to stop jerking off, but I can't. I can't stand. I can't do anything other than stroke it.

Mr. Smith is only three rows away. Under his breath he is muttering "penis." My anxiety level is off the chart.

The room turns red and I start screaming and ejaculating. The whole class is watching as Mr. Smith slams down my copy of the test with his right hand and swiftly tears off my penis with his left.

And then we are all laughing, and I don't feel anxious anymore. I think that maybe it's ok that my penis is gone. Just another scar.

Wax Lips Opiates

From his corner of the sewer the universe was populated by unbelievable creatures.

The Syringimals were filled to their 60 ml capacity with a gelatinous ocher blood. They fluttered around using sparkly wings stolen from Disney fairies, and attempted language through wax lips that were usually secured with scotch tape.

His morning ritual was to somehow lift his incredibly huge head up from a crack-smothered mattress. This task used to be easy. A curious baby only a few months old could do it. But, as his body still inverted in on itself and his head still continued to expand, he began needing the help of the fluttering druggie equipment.

They sensed his need and were there for him. As soon as his leaded eyelids cranked open, even a little, three or four of them were there, tapping for veins with their lips in an awkward, drunken hummingbird dance. They slid in the needles as soon as they struck gold and patiently waited for him to plunge each one in order. For those few moments, as they anticipated his awakening, the Syringimals rested, and the universe sighed.

You're All Knuckles

Her eyeballs are made of fur, like plush little bumble-bees at home in her sockets.

She's talking about process. About building the world's greatest rocking chair. About climbing the walls of her apartment with nothing but a spatula coated in Nutella.

I hear her. She's making sense.

I want to rip off her clothes but they're made of some gelatinous mess that only gives up one wet handful at a time. This is funny to her but not so funny to me.

I think back on a life of sexual frustration. She must be the goddess that made my exploits so miserable.

This is what she says before slipping through a hatch in the floor: You're all knuckles.

The Eric Dolphy Marching Band

My wife storms into the kitchen with a pink mako shark slung over her shoulder, barking "Dinner!" towards me as I sit on the counter swishing my middle finger through a bowl of sand.

Outside of the screen door a marching band of fifteen Eric Dolphy clones hops down the street in unison, passing their black saxophones back and forth like hot potatoes.

She slams the shark down onto the kitchen island like she's hammering a railroad stake. A cloud of pink gas squirts from its gills in the key of E.

"Is it dead?" I ask, finding a small decoder ring in the sand.

"Of course it is," my wife huffs. "Do you think I'd be able to drag a live shark all the way up the hill?"

"I'm just amazed that you can carry it at all."

She ignores me and unsheathes an impossibly long machete from her pocket. I try not to gag as she expertly goes about disemboweling the slimy creature.

Hot guts pile up around her skinny bare ankles.

"I'll save a tooth for you, like always," she remarks, licking blood off the tip of the blade. The Eric Dolphy Marching Band retreats backwards, retracing their steps up the street.

Buy Me Some Peanuts

The phone rings as I begin to saw into the crisped socks with a translucent steak knife, and I curse my luck by shoving the TV tray to the carpet. David Lee Roth calls a halt to the band from the other side of the flat screen and asks me directly what the fuck my problem is.

"Hungry!" I scream, raising my fists in the air.

The air in my living room vibrates again with the second blare from the rotary phone. I stomp over and snatch it impatiently, too angry to say anything. The voice on the other end mumbles, not forming words, but I understand: I am to be the starting third baseman for the Detroit Tigers.

(())

I don't know if there is actually a ballpark in Niger, why the Tigers are in town, who they are playing, what time the first pitch is to be thrown, or anything else pertinent to being a baseball player on this particular afternoon.

I find a small man pushing a wheelbarrow loaded with baseball gloves. He must know something.

"Are you going to the game?" I ask, my voice quivering with anxiety.

"Of course! Hop on!" He waves to the pile of leather and I climb up, sitting like a nervous dog as the man weaves his way through vendors, broken-down vehicles, and lost donkeys.

(())

The small man deposits me in front of a small brick building where two women are poised motionless over a chess board in the display window.

"Angry!" I bellow, standing precariously on the mountain of gloves, which has grown to the height of a small elephant. A crack of thunder pops behind my shaking fists while the clouds open up and shower the earth with perfectly prepared crisped socks.

Living Through Fuzzy

They politely urged him not to get too involved with his creations.

Breathing life into Fuzzy, he couldn't help but smile. A geyser of joy, an erection of bliss. A seed taking root.

Fuzzy was number sixty-eight. So many more to go, but he didn't want to continue. He held Fuzzy in his arms and wished to be like him. He wished to be what he had made.

His celestial colleagues shook their shiny heads when he relinquished his power and climbed into Fuzzy through the velcro pocket. The measure of a soul is the greatness of its inventions.

Traveling across Earth, he relished the feel of dirt under his soles.

Now is the time to make babies. Now is the time to focus on survival. Now is the time for candy and musk.

Looking up, he saw death for the first time.

Shit shit shit, he fumed. I should have thought this through.

Chocolate Dog

My ghost has already been places I'll never see. Listen to my bones: Special Reports. Tales from the dark side. A universe cut from light exploding on a printmaker's fist. My house is your house is built by radio signals beamed from the bottom of the ocean. This is peace, I found it swimming between us, two lonely fish full of questions. You are my future but I am your past, we can only meet between staccato notes. I'm dead, sucking on a chocolate dog, feeling it out for the last time.

Sorbet in the Luminous Capsule

What a dream. The excellent heart-firework. The future gold, a moving mannequin.

You turn to me, head smaller than ever. Fading into itself. I wonder if this is what self-redaction feels like. "Sorbet," you say, sounding like an echo.

"Is that ok?" I ask.

Now your head is flickering, losing the signal. I slow the process and find myself staring with wet eyes at a headless you. These moments last forever, and I file them away.

Off to fetch the sorbet, leaving you alone on the grass. Privacy settings are high; only a dozen or so of the thousands present are actually visible. One of them is just a pair of moon boots, hopping toward the bushes, another a shadow folding over the lawn. Above, the Theta district of the park silently rolls, its distance itself romantic and awesome. Several jumpers have died already this year attempting to bridge the gap, decked out like birds, crowds trailing with their feeds. Sometimes bodies just vanish, their privacy commandeered by shadows. I'm surprised they still try.

Returning, your head is embedded in a slow loop. Face/Void protocol. I'm enraptured. Even in the brief flickers where your eyes and nose are visible you look gelatinous. Like a forgotten traveler suctioned to the side of an immersion tank. Am I sick because this bizarre spectacle is irresistible to me?

I love you. I say it, I think. Or maybe I just subvocalized it. Do I want you to hear me say it?

"Sssss...baaay."

I almost forgot. One purple scoop. With no mouth to eat it.

I begin to count time in my head. Sync it with your binary reality. Your head. Quickly, I slip the sorbet where your mouth was a nanosecond before, and release, yanking my hands upwards.

Success almost happens before it happens. I don't have to wait. You are whole, pushing the cold lump around your mouth in satisfaction.

"S'good," you mumble.

1-Up

"I believe in the redemptive power of bacon. I believe in the redemptive power of pork," says the Rooster, backing me into the corner of the pen, his pink eyes glowing through the reflection of an Eastbound dust storm.

Behind me the pigs huddle together, shivering collectively. The air smells like dream, like farm shit, like the salty stalling of evolution. There is a small ax in my left hand, but I don't intend to slaughter with it. I don't even want it, yet the Rooster chills me so intensely that before he can sidle any closer I fling it at him, splitting him clean in two. The pigs squeal and vomit, as do I, as does the sky, dust rushing in sooner than expected.

From the parted and equal halves of the Rooster a shiny cartoonish green mushroom sprouts, WOOBWOOBWOOBWOOB! It glides along the mud of the pen, bouncing off the fence as the pigs laugh and give chase.

I don't need another life. This one is enough. Walking away I idly kick a turtle, who retreats into his shell, flops on his back, and speeds away, knocking out three other strolling turtles on his way to the flagpole.

What it Means to Exodus, or,
BRAAAAAAWWWW

"I have consulted the Internet," the man remarks, squatting low, sorting through a mountain of tablets. He snags two and stands slowly, confidently, and I realize suddenly that he is Moses. Two iPads, cradled surely in each wrist, glow with lists.

"I have not read the Bible, but I know what it means to exodus," he pontificates.

"Exodus can't be a verb, right?" Says the man next to me. He looks impossibly old, a fleshy statue made of thin wood. A totem pole.

Moses ignores him and continues. "The almighty Google, that which knows the answer before you finish the question, which knows millions of answers in fact. That which provides us with every possible answer to every possible question...which is billions upon billions of answers!"

My head is dissolving, filling with space.

Moses increases his volume. "And you know what an infinite, uncountable number of answers equals?"

"Not a fucking thing," whispers the old wooden man, conspiratorially.

"Not a fucking thing!" Moses whoops, pretending that he said it first.

I can feel the space in my brain, fueled by subtle electricity. Lots of different electricities, mingling at every potential level. The dream is suddenly more real than real.

Moses fixes his eyes upon me, and prods his finger into my chest, except he's standing ten feet away, separated by a few motionless people. "You," he says. "You know what it means to exodus, don't you? You're already gone, eh? More absent than present?"

I try to speak, but my lips seem to be encased in a thick dough. "Brrrraaaawww," I say.

"BRRRRAAAAWWW!" Moses mimics, laughing and slapping his knee, and he starts swearing incredulously. Yet the air is suddenly bbbbrrrraaawwwing of its own accord. I join, but I'm not laughing. No, I think I'm gonna drown.

The senses make their exodus. The words on the tablet are nonsense, commanding nothing. All religion is silly.

Brrrraaaawww.

The Finding Smile

He was a smile. The rest of him was almost transparent, barely a glimmer of form, but his gaping grin shone so intensely that it provided a distraction from everything else missing.

My mother gave her all to convince him to be a politician. My sister begged on bleeding knees for him to give her head. I just needed somebody to help me find things.

I handed him the list of lost items. He quickly looked it over, then swallowed it whole with that magnificent, glowing mouth. "We'll look for your sense of humor first," he said.

It took six days in the jungle until we finally had leads. He negotiated with birds so colorful they made crayons leap from cliffs. He threatened enormous snakes, and when they didn't cooperate he'd clench their jaws between his gleaming teeth and swing them around like weed whackers.

We finally stumbled upon the End of the Earth. A beautiful sight for sure, the red yolk of sun framing his levitating smile, bright upon brighter. Hovering closer, he whispered "Look in your pants. The secret to humor is nestled softly down there."

So we began the frightful journey back home. By law I was required to go without my trousers or underwear. To refuse would invalidate the rediscovery of comedy. He took hold of my shaft and used it to point us toward the highway.

In this way he guided us out of the jungle and home to my wife, where I proceeded to make love to her with all kinds of sarcastic thrusts. Orgasmic laughter all around. "I'm sure glad you followed that smile," she later sighed, sweat dripping from her chin to her clavicle.

Infinite Penis

He finds a beach ball and recreates humanity upon it. Kicking it down the shore he wonders how the little people must feel about each other. To place them on such a tiny globe almost seems unfair.

The only way to make himself real is to spawn others that believe in him. He sweats and watches the bouncing boobs of the women who gather around him. It's hard to restrain his erection.

When his pants explode his penis is let loose with the force of a sonic boom. The women faint and his ball explodes into a million fluttering scraps. He weeps as the little people fall to the ground.

It will take him years to reel in his infinite penis, which he must do carefully. He's too shaken. Nobody else should share the fate of his beach ball children.

Shawn Misener lives and writes in Michigan.
Since 2007 he has had over 250 stories and poems
published, both in print and online. He is currently
finishing work on his first novel.

MORE ROADSIDE PRESS TITLES

MORE ROADSIDE PRESS TITLES

MORE ROADSIDE PRESS TITLES